SUMI'S PRIZE

Pictures by

KAZUE
MIZUMURA

Sumi's Prize

By

YOSHIKO UCHIDA

CHARLES SCRIBNER'S SONS

NEW YORK

In remembrance of my grandmothers

賞状
人命救助ノ
功ヲ彰ス
消防署長
印

一等賞

賞
競技

特賞
植村須佐男
太ノ者技能卓越
ニシテ成績優透
之ヲ彰ス
昭和三十六年二月六
刀村田ヲ球長
大石久良助
印

佳作
太ノ多音画
以和

Just once Sumi wanted to win a prize. Even a tiny prize would do, for Sumi had never won a prize for anything in her whole life. Now she was seven and in the second grade at the village school. She did not want to grow old without ever having done something wonderful enough to deserve a prize.

She simply had to win a prize before another year went by. But what could she do? She couldn't even win a gold star in her notebook for good work. Always she made a mistake, or her thumb left a big black smudge on the corner of a page.

"Someday you will have a gold star," her teacher told her. "Just keep trying."

Sumi did try, but it was no use. She tried especially hard because her teacher was so special. He had a round bald head and wore glasses shaped like small half-moons. But that was not why he was special. He was special because he was also the mayor of Sugi Village and everyone called him Mr. Mayor. He was the only person in the village who owned a shiny black top hat.

It was a gift from the Governor and it was his Mayor's Hat. It went on his head to all the village weddings and funerals and festivals, and the mayor kept it in a cupboard at school.

Sometimes when no one was looking, Sumi would get on a chair and touch the hat which felt as silky as a black cat.

On days when he felt more like a mayor than a teacher, Mr. Mayor would wear the hat in the classroom. Then he would give out gold stars and shake the hands of the pupils who won them. Sumi thought he looked like a prime minister giving out medals from the Emperor, and more than ever she wanted to do something wonderful and have him shake her hand.

"Someday that will happen," her mother said.

"Someday you may win a prize," her father added.

Her big brother Taro kept quiet, however, for he didn't think Sumi could ever win anything. After all, she was only seven, and she was a girl.

One day, when the rice was harvested and the days were growing cold, Mr. Mayor made an announcement at school.

"Harrumph," he said, clearing his throat. "There will be a kite flying contest on the banks of the river on New Year's Day. There will be a prize for the best and most beautiful kite." Then he tapped his head as though his top hat were sitting on it and added, "I shall be the judge."

Sumi's hand flew up. "Can girls enter?" she asked.

The boys began to laugh. "Girls can't fly kites," they muttered.

But Mr. Mayor rubbed his chin and thought about
it. "Why not?" he said slowly. "The contest is open to
all the children of the village."

At last, a chance to win a prize! Sumi was very good at folding paper cranes and flowers. She was sure she could make a good kite with a little help from Father. She would make the most beautiful kite in all the village and she would win the prize. The more she thought of it, the more Sumi felt she could win. She felt it down to the tip of her big toe, and that was a good sign.

There was one problem, however, and that was her brother Taro. He would enter the contest too and if Father helped him as well, his kite would be better, for they had made many beautiful kites together. Sumi was worried, but that night Taro gave her a nice surprise.

"I'm making my kite alone," he announced. After all, he was ten and could do a few things for himself.

So Sumi began to work on her kite. First she drew the design on a piece of paper. The kite would be in the shape of a great butterfly and she would paint it gold and black. She went to the stationers to buy string and paint and the proper kind of paper. Sumi worked hard for many days and when she was ready, Mother cooked some starch to make the paste.

Then Father helped her put the kite together.
"The kite must be light and it must be strong,"
Father said. "And it must be properly balanced."

Sumi made three kites before she finally made one that was just right. Then Father went with her to the river's edge to try it out. On the very first try, Sumi's golden butterfly soared into the sky as though that was where it belonged. Sumi watched it happily and shouted, "I'm going to win the prize!"

But when Taro finished his kite, she was not so sure. His kite was sturdy and bold with the face of a *samurai* warrior glaring from it in purple, red and yellow. It looked fierce enough to batter down Sumi's butterfly.

If only both of us could win, Sumi thought. But she knew very well there was only one prize.

Now that her kite was ready, Sumi could scarcely wait for New Year's Day. She waited and she worried as the first snows came and left the ground laced with patches of white. But when New Year's Day came at last, the weather was bright and clear and exactly right for flying kites.

Sumi put on her new silk *kimono*. "Happy New Year!" she called. "Today is the day of the contest!"

"Well, well, so it is," Father said, as though he had forgotten.

Mother had prepared all sorts of wonderful things for their special New Year's breakfast. Sumi liked the toasted rice cakes best, but Taro liked the knotted seaweed.

Then it was time to go to the shrine to ask for the blessings of a good year. Sumi said her prayers as fast as she could and ran home ahead of the others. She took off her *kimono*, folded it carefully and put it away. *Kimonos* were all right for saying New Year prayers but not for flying kites.

Sumi hurried into her warm slacks and her big
woolly sweater. She took the red bows from her hair
and tied her braids back so they would not flop in her
face. She put new laces in her sneakers so she would
not trip as she ran with her kite. She inspected her kite
over and over again to make sure it had not come loose
anywhere. Then she was ready.

After lunch they all started for the river bank where
the contest would be held. Mother looked at the bright,
clear sky. "A fresh new day for the new year," she
said cheerfully.

Taro ran ahead to look at the kites his friends had
made.

Sumi walked with Father. She held her golden butterfly in one hand and her father's hand in the other. The closer they got to the river, the more her feet seemed to want to turn around and go home. She looked up at Father, but he seemed eager to reach the river bank. "The wind is just right," he said.

There were already many people at the river's edge
when they arrived, and Sumi saw the girls in her class.
They all wore gay silk *kimonos* and bows in their hair.
Not one was wearing slacks and sneakers. Not one was
holding a kite. Sumi swallowed hard. She was the only
girl in the whole village to enter the contest.

Sumi saw Mr. Mayor in his black frock coat, his striped trousers and his shiny top hat. She had not seen him look so elegant since the day he was elected mayor. He stood at a table draped with red and white bunting and bowed as he wished everyone a happy new year.

Now the boys lined up in front of him with their kites, and Mother urged Sumi along.

"Good luck!" she whispered.

Sumi found a place at the end of the line and looked anxiously at the other kites. There were all kinds of kites, and they were all sizes and shapes. One was square and another was diamond-shaped. One was a hollowed-out box and another was a snowman. Some

were decorated with many colors and some were painted with dragons, for this was the first day of the Year of the Dragon. No one had a warrior as fierce as Taro's. And no one had a golden butterfly. Sumi thought hers was the most beautiful kite of them all.

Mr. Mayor walked up and down inspecting the kites. "Very fine," he murmured. "Very fine."

He paused for a moment in front of Sumi and nodded. "Ah," he said, but that was all.

Sumi wanted to tell him how hard she had worked on her kite, but her tongue wouldn't move. She wanted to wish him a happy new year, but all she could do was scratch the tip of her nose.

Then it was time to get the kites up. Father helped Sumi get her butterfly into the air and then it was all up to her. Carefully, carefully, she let out the string, tugging to keep her butterfly climbing higher and higher.

"Climb! Climb!" Sumi shouted to her butterfly.

It seemed to hear her, for it soared up and up, straight toward the sun. From the corner of her eye, Sumi could see Taro's warrior. It was soaring too, but her butterfly was going higher. It truly was. Sumi knew that she would win, for if she could beat Taro, she knew she could beat anybody. Now, at last, she would have her prize!

Sumi glanced at Mr. Mayor to be sure that he saw her kite. He was watching it with his head tipped back, shading his eyes from the sun. And then it happened! A gust of wind swooped along the bank of the river and swept his top hat right off his head. It went whirling along the sand straight toward the water.

"My hat!" Mr. Mayor shouted. "My hat!"

"Stop!" Sumi shouted. But the hat was such a nice round shape for rolling, it just whirled on and on.

"Mr. Mayor's hat!" Sumi called out. But everyone was too busy looking up to notice what was going on below.

It was hard to watch her kite and the hat as well, but Sumi knew she must help Mr. Mayor. Now the hat was at the water's edge and Sumi had to save it. She took one last look at her golden butterfly and then, holding tight to its string, she ran as fast as she could.

She threw herself on the hat with a great thud and felt it flatten beneath her. She had saved the hat, but she had squashed it flat. Worse still, she had given her kite such a jerk, it turned upside down and came tumbling from the sky. Like a wounded bird, her golden butterfly zigzagged to earth and crumpled in a heap on the sand.

"Ohhhhh." A sad cry rippled through the crowd like a winter wind, for now everyone saw what had happened.

Mr. Mayor ran to Sumi's side. "Are you all right, little one?" he asked, and he helped her to her feet.

Sumi nodded, but she could not keep back her tears. "My kite's broken," she said sadly, "and I squashed your hat."

Mr. Mayor looked sad too. "I am sorry about your kite," he said. "It was a fine kite. But don't worry about my hat." He knew a few things about top hats that Sumi didn't know.

"Watch," he said, and he whacked the hat on his arm. It popped up with a zing, looking as though it had never been under Sumi's stomach at all. Mr. Mayor put the hat back on his head and took Sumi's hand.

"Come with me," he said, and he led her to the judging table with the red and white bunting.

Mother and Father hurried to Sumi's side. "Are you all right?" they asked. "We saw you save Mr. Mayor's hat!" they added proudly.

The mayor let Sumi sit beside him at the table, and like two solemn judges they watched the bright kites speckle the holiday sky.

Sumi saw Taro's warrior soaring above all the others and she knew he would win. Now he would have the prize while she still had none. Sumi wanted to cry. She had come so close to winning.

Soon it was time to pull down the kites and the Mayor asked everyone to gather around. The prize was a beautiful box of water-color paints and everyone clapped when it went to Taro, for his kite had truly flown best of all. The contest was over and people began to drift away.

Mr. Mayor, however, was not finished. "Just a moment," he said, and he fumbled about in his pockets. Finally he pulled out his big blue fountain pen.

"I seem to have another prize," he said. "It is for the only girl to enter the contest and the only person in Sugi Village to rescue a top hat from the river!"

Then the mayor, wearing his beautiful top hat, shook Sumi's hand and gave her his own fountain pen.

Sumi was sure she must be dreaming. Everyone clapped and cheered. They were glad there was another prize for Sumi. The girls from her class crowded about her wanting to take turns holding the pen in their hands.

"The mayor's own pen!" they said in excited voices. "That's the best prize there ever was."

Later at home, Father said, "Well, Sumi, you did win a prize after all."

"It is not every family that wins two prizes in one day," Mother added. "I will make some red bean rice to celebrate."

Even Taro wanted to be nice. "That was a pretty good kite," he said, "for a girl's."

Sumi could not find words for the big happiness inside her. That night she took the fountain pen to bed and put it beside her pillow. Then she closed her eyes and remembered the whole wonderful day. She could still see all the kites dancing in the sky, and she could see the mayor smiling in his top hat and shaking

her hand. Suddenly, Sumi knew that she no longer needed to worry about winning anything, for today she had done something no one else in Sugi Village could ever do again. In fact, who in all of Japan could enter a kite contest and win the mayor's own fountain pen for saving his hat? Nobody, Sumi thought happily, nobody but me!